GROWING PANGS

GROWING PANGS

KATHRYN ORMSBEE

ILLUSTRATED BY

MOLLY BROOKS

WITH COLOR BY BEX GLENDINING AND ELISE SCHUENKE

RANDOM HOUSE 🏠 NEW YORK

Text copyright © 2022 by Kathryn Ormsbee
Jacket art and interior illustrations copyright © 2022 by Molly Brooks

All rights reserved. Published in the United States by Random House Children's Books, a division of Penguin Random House LLC, New York.

Random House and the colophon are registered trademarks of Penguin Random House LLC. RH Graphic with the book design is a trademark of Penguin Random House LLC.

Photographs on pp. 243 and 245 from the personal collection of Kathryn Ormsbee, used by permission.

Visit us on the Web! rhcbooks.com

Educators and librarians, for a variety of teaching tools, visit us at RHTeachersLibrarians.com

Library of Congress Cataloging-in-Publication Data is available upon request.
ISBN 978-0-593-30128-9 (hardcover) | ISBN 978-0-593-30131-9 (trade pbk.)
ISBN 978-0-593-30129-6 (lib. bdg.) | ISBN 978-0-593-30130-2 (ebook)

Interior design by Molly Brooks and April Ward

MANUFACTURED IN CHINA
10 9 8 7 6 5 4 3 2 1
First Edition

To Beth Phelan, who has been
an agent extraordinaire these
eight years and who encouraged me
to try something new and scary,
like writing a graphic novel

—K.O.

For my parents

—M.B.

Kacey and I had met two years earlier at our weekly homeschool co-op.

WELCOME BACK, BLUEGRASS HOMESCHOOL CO-OP!

We hit it off right away.

Hey! Our names sound cool together. Like a band.

Katie

Kacey

We both loved books.

Have you read the new Royal Diaries book about Anastasia?

YES. I wonder if she really escaped the Bolsheviks.

Right? She could still be alive in France or someplace!

You're NEVER FULLY DRESSED WITHOUT A SMILE!

We were obsessed with the musical Annie.

3

And we were both homeschooled.

BLUEGRASS HOMESCHOOL CO-OP

estoy   estamos
estás   estáis
está   están

So I didn't feel like the weirdo homeschooled kid when Kacey and I hung out.

Wait. You two don't go to *real* school?

WEIRDOS!

HA HA HA HA HA HA HA HA

I did school at home for most of the week, but Fridays were co-op days.

That's when I went to classes like Spanish, art, drama, and gym with other homeschoolers.

6

7

8

I know older kids from church who've gone. They say it's *awesome.*

And there's a giant pool?

Uh-huh. And a zip line and a campfire, *and* there's a big talent show at the end of the week.

It sounds *really* cool.

When I asked my parents about Camp Aldridge . . .

. . . they said I could go!

But a few weeks later . . .

You've been quiet tonight, Katiebug.

I'm a little worried, I guess.

About camp.

That makes sense.

It does?

Sure. Overnight camp is a big deal.

It's only natural you're nervous.

Dad and I will be a phone call away.

And you'll have Kacey there with you.

Yeah.

x

11

Hey, um . . . Ashley?

Uh-huh.

You've been to camp before, right?

Yeah.

It's not a big deal.

You'll forget you were nervous after the first day.

Okay.

I wanted to talk more about it.

But I didn't want Ashley thinking I was scared.

I wanted to be like Ashley one day.

Pretty and cool and confident.

Right now, though?

Compared to Ashley, I felt like a little kid.

But Camp Aldridge was a chance to prove I was mature.

I can do this.

I couldn't swat away a buzzing feeling in my brain.

What if you miss home too much?

So much that you can't fall asleep at night?

What if you do something super embarrassing in front of the whole camp?

Or you get sick, and Mom's not there to take care of you?

This wasn't the first time I'd gotten buzzing thoughts.

They'd started a few years ago.

Lately, though, I'd been getting them more and more.

Bzz Bzz Bzzz Bzz Bzn Bzn

They told me what to do, like a big, buzzing bully.

You gotta make your worries stop.

BZZZ BZZ BZ BZ BZ BZ

Move that zipper.

BZZZZ

If I moved the zipper, camp would be fun. Nothing bad would happen.

You just have to move it three more times.

Hey.

What're you doing?

Um.

Nothing.

Okay, cool. I thought your backpack was broken.

How bad would *that* be on our first day of camp?

Yeah. Totally.

I left my backpack alone after that.

BZzz

BZzz

But the buzzing thoughts didn't go away.

Welcome to Camp Aldridge! We're so happy you're here.

EEEEEEE♡E!E!E!

22

23

I call
bottom bunk!

Okay, Katie,
that means you
get . . .

. . . the top
bunk.

gulp.

25

I'll let you girls get settled. Dinner is at the mess hall in thirty minutes!

Hey, Kacey?

Would you maybe wanna switch beds?

Why?

I couldn't admit that I was scared I'd fall off in the middle of the night.

Poof!

I'm just used to sleeping closer to the ground.

BZZ BZZ

Well, then it's more of an adventure to sleep on the top bunk, right?

BZZ

Yeah, I guess so.

Let's head over to the mess hall!

The counselors sing before dinner, and it's *hilarious.*

Oh, yeah! Um . . .

You go ahead. I'll catch up.

If you're sure. I'll save a spot for you.

The buzzing thoughts were bad.

They told me that if I made my bed *just so* . . .

Tuck!

BZZ

Tuck

. . . I wouldn't fall off in the middle of the night.

Stuff that makes me
Different

red hair→

• homeschooled

• supercrooked
teeth (going
to get braces
next month)

• young for
my grade

tons of
freckles

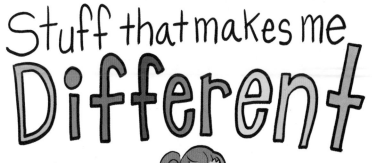

I didn't want to add buzzing thoughts to that list.

I had to keep cool and not act like a kid. I had to—

HEY!

TAP

M—me?

Yeah, *you.*

My name's Delaney. You headed to dinner?

Yeah! I'm Katie.

Delaney is such a cool name.

32

So what grade are you going into?

Sixth.

Sweet! Me too. Where do you go?

Uh-oh. One of the things that makes me different . . .

I go to school in Lexington.

That's not exactly a lie.

Oh. I live in Bowling Green.

That's pretty far from here.

Yeah, it's basically Tennessee.

MESS HALL

So what's your favorite band?

Mine is *NSYNC.

I wonder where Kacey is.

You gotta choose an alliance: *NSYNC or Backstreet Boys.

But Backstreet Boys *suck*.

Lance is pretty cute, but Joey is *so old*. Like, a dinosaur. And then there's Chris and JC, who I'm just like "meh" about.

Sooo, who do you like?

Whoa. Delaney cusses. I'm not allowed to say "suck."

And I don't know *any* members of *NSYNC.

34

I like musicals. You know, like *The Phantom of the Opera?* Or *Annie?*

Huh. Interesting.

Who're you looking for?

My friend . . .

. . . KACEY!

Isn't this place awesome?

I grabbed you a glow-in-the-dark lanyard! They were running out.

Thanks!

Delaney, this is my best friend, Kacey.

So you two go to the same school?

Actually, we're . . .

Oh no. Don't say it.

. . . homeschooled.

NOOooooooooo

Oh. That's . . . interesting.

I got the feeling that when Delaney said "interesting" she really meant "uncool."

Giggle

HA HA

But Delaney was cool.

That's the best spot in the house!

Hey, Delaney!

What's up, Delaney?

And confident.

We were here first, dudes. Back off!

She knew lots of stuff I didn't, about music and movies and *life*.

I'll have to show you how I do mascara.

It's a trick I learned from *Cosmopolitan*.

And oh my God, do you ever think about how we could be in a real-life *Friday the 13th*?

Like, Jason could be watching us right now.

Delaney can watch R-rated movies?

I call it EXTREME FIZZ. You gotta put in every single soda flavor.

Ew, gross!

...but cool.

You know what would be awesome? Synchronized swimming in the pool!

Oooh, yeah. We should try it.

Sounds fine, I guess.

We could be our own fellowship.

The fellowship of . . . the bracelet!

S-s-sure!

Awesome!

See ya!

MESS HALL

Bye!

41

Even though I got homesick every so often...

CANNONBALL

...it was nothing a little camp fun couldn't fix.

My sister, Ashley, says I should enjoy stuff like this while I can.

She says you can't eat marshmallow *anything* when you have braces.

That sucks. You nervous about getting them?

Kind of. I'm mainly worried I'll look weird.

Oh. You definitely will.

But if anyone can pull off a brace face, it's you.

You're spending too much time with Delaney.

We're just hanging out.

But camp was my idea.

You should be spending more time with me.

If you're friends with Delaney, you're, like, betraying our friendship.

I hadn't meant to betray Kacey.

I'd just been having fun with Delaney, too.

Check it out. It's the new Weezer album.

My sister likes them!

She plays them in her bathroom all the time.

She's got the same Walkman as you, too.

47

It was different, being friends with Delaney.

She was more like Ashley than like Kacey.

More . . . grown-up.

Well, how come you don't like them?

Too deep for you?

What if Delaney thinks I'm *not* grown-up? Not cool enough?

I forgot you like *musicals.* Cute, fluffy stuff like that.

No! I like this kind of music, too.

BZZ

BZZ

I just have to save up for my own CDs, and that can take a while.

CABIN

Well, you can borrow mine whenever.

That's what the fellowship of the bracelet is for.

The buzzing thoughts wouldn't leave me alone.

They told me I would feel better if I did certain things.

Like retie my shoes, even when they were perfectly tied.

Go on without me! I'll catch up!

. . . eight, nine, ten.

Whoa! Easy there.

Or tap the dispensers a certain number of times when I was making an Extreme Fizz.

I knew deep down that those buzzing thoughts were silly.

But sometimes they were all I could hear.

CAMP ALDRIDGE TALENT SHOW

On the last day of camp, Kacey and I sang a duet.

YOU'RE NEVER fully dressed without a SMILE!

But she wasn't totally happy with me.

GOODBYE, CAMPERS

Delaney and I were bummed, too.

I wish you didn't live so far from Lexington.

It majorly sucks.

Call me whenever.

Yeah. And if homeschool kids get school pictures, send me one.

I wanna see what you look like as a brace face.

Remember: The fellowship of the bracelet will endure!

Kacey and I wouldn't be riding home together.

Her family was going to Canada for three weeks.

That meant Kacey would be gone on the first day of homeschool co-op.

And she still seemed mad about Delaney.

I hoped that when she got home from vacation, everything would go back to normal.

Have fun up north!

Poof!

She was wearing her necklace at least.

On the ride home, I opened and shut my locket ten times in a row.

CLICK

BZZZ

You're an official overnight camper.

It's old hat now!

The buzzing thoughts told me that if I did that, I wouldn't lose my best friend.

CLICK

CLICK

BZZZZz

I was home, and it was the end of summer.

Since Kacey wasn't around, I had lots of free time.

Sometimes I snuck into Ashley's room to look at her magazines.

Hmm.

You want your hair chopped, huh?

Well, you gotta promise not to cry about it in the morning.

Promise.

SNiP!

SNiP

All right. Ready?

I'd made a huge mistake. And even worse?

The next day was my big orthodontist appointment.

Poof!

BZz

BZzz z

The buzzing thoughts told me I had to turn my bedside lamp on and off . . .

CLICK

. . . until I finally felt okay.

... something unusual ...

... worried about ...

What's unusual?

Katie, why don't you come over here?

You see, the string beneath your tongue is very short.

Back in the old days, you would've been called "tongue-tied."

BZZZZ

BZzz

BZZ

65

You may have already encountered some problems, like mild speech difficulty and trouble swallowing.

There's a risk that these difficulties could grow worse over time.

What I'd suggest is talking to your dentist about a lingual frenectomy.

Surgery.

Thank you. I'll get in touch with our dentist right away.

M–Mom, I don't want surgery.

My tongue is fine.

Dad and I will only consider surgery if Dr. Kramer recommends it.

Even if they have to do the procedure, it won't be a big deal.

It sure felt like a big deal, though.

BZZZ

Tongue . . . tongue.

BZZZZZZB

Tongue, tongue, tongue.

BZZZ

The buzzing thoughts told me that if I whispered the word "tongue" enough, the surgery wouldn't happen.

Tongue. Tongue. Tongue.

BZZZZ

UP TO 60% off

BUY 2 GET 1 50%

BZZZ BZZZ BZZZZ

Tongue.

Tongue, tongue.

BZZZZZZ

Poof

Are you ready for school, hon?

Yes, ma'am.

And where do you go?

Oh. I see.

I'm homeschooled.

That's *such a* disservice to your child. How will she learn to socialize?

Oh, I think she'll manage.

Have a nice day!

Plus, I liked to work at my own pace at home.

And I didn't have to worry about homework at night.

I didn't think those adults knew what homeschooling was actually like for me.

First day of co-cop!

First day of middle school.

First day of—wait.

Is that . . .

A PIMPLE?

I bet even a few of your friends will have them.

Poof

It's not as bad as you think. People will hardly notice.

BZzz

But to me, that pimple was my worst enemy.

BZZ BZZ ZZZ

BZZZ ZzZz BZZ ZZ BZ

Haha! I'm gonna make sixth grade the *worst*.

I tried to focus on good things, like seeing my friends and filling my brand-new binder with notes.

Katie!

Hey!

Lauren
Megan ↓ Callie

No one said a thing about my pimple. They were all too excited about . . .

. . . the *new girl.*

This is Jaime! She just started homeschooling this year.

Nice to meet you.

We have the same binder!

Guess we both have good taste.

Oh, hey, they're starting opening ceremonies.

Wanna sit together?

Definitely. I can show you around since it's your first day.

I love theatre. I was in lots of plays at my old school.

We did a production of *A Midsummer Night's Dream* that was set in the 1920s, and I got to be a flapper named Helena.

That's so cool!

Jaime reminded me a little of Delaney: She was cool and outgoing, but she wasn't as . . . *intense*.

And she was homeschooled, so I didn't have to worry that she'd make fun of me or not understand.

It looks fixable.

I hope so.

BZZZZ

Hanging out with Jaime was fun.

Jellicles DO! AND Jellicles CAN!

But I missed Kacey.

TORONTO

Greetings from MONTRÉAL

83

KNOCK KNOCK

BZZ ZZ

Come in!

BZZ

BZZ-ZZ

Don't worry, Katiebug. Nothing I can't fix.

POOF

The next week, I was so *excited* to see Kacey at co-op. But when I showed up . . .

. . . Kacey wasn't there yet.

Katie! Hey!

Come sit with us?

Good morning, BHC! Let's get started with some special announcements.

What should I do? I can't get up now.

Sorry!

Your necklace.

Oh. It broke. My dad's fixing it, though.

Hey, Kacey!

Hey!

Hey, y'all.

Whatever. We're gonna be late for class.

POOF

BZZzzz

BZZZZzz

So did you speak French in Montreal?

A little.

I've been working on a new theme park on RollerCoaster Tycoon.

Uh-huh.

I got tired of the one-sided conversation, so I talked to my other friends instead.

giggle

Until . . .

IMPROV DAY!

Katie and Kacey, you pair up.

"You are actors on a Broadway stage."

Annie.

Somehow, our improv made everything better.

Kacey stopped giving me the cold shoulder.

♪ You're Never Fully Dressed without a Smile! ♪

PROV AY

HA HA HA HA

Hey!

poof

That was so good, you two.

Thanks!

Kacey, this is Jaime.

Jaime, this is my best friend, Kacey.

Cool. Nice to meet you.

You too.

poof

Everything was back to normal, the way it had been before camp.

91

I'm pretty sure it's "Hard-Knock Life."

Like...

KNOCK

That doesn't make sense. What does "hard knock" even mean?

I dunno, it's just a saying.

What does "hard not" mean?

You know, like all the stuff the orphans aren't:

Not rich,

not loved,

not cared for.

I still think it's *knock.*

It's *not.*

Whatever.

Doesn't matter. I'll be the one singing the reprise, since I'm playing Annie.

Wh—what?

Well, that's what we were thinking, right?

I've got the most experience, since I played Esther in my church's play last year.

Well, yeah, but... I can sing.

And I have red hair, like Annie.

But you don't have any actual theatre experience.

That's not fair.

You don't just get to be Annie.

Annie
the musical
(the sequel)

Well, neither do you!

This is boring, anyway.

Let's watch TV instead.

Poof

Things were getting weird again with Kacey, and I didn't know how to fix them.

It's the HARD KNOCK LIFE for US!

I was right!

Who are you talking to?

N—no one.

I was excited for my first slumber party of the school year.

But then . . .

Kacey got so upset at camp about Delaney.

What if she starts feeling that way about Jaime, too?

Did you eject the movie from the VCR?

If you didn't, something bad will happen. The house will catch fire, or you'll break your arm, or . . . Kacey will stop being friends with you.

Forever.

You'd better do something about it. NOW.

Everything's going to be the way it used to be.

The next week, before co-op, I checked on my necklace.

Sorry, Katiebug.

I've been swamped with work. I promise I'll fix it by next week, though, okay?

Okay.

I can't wait for you all to come over.

I found this cool candy recipe, and my mom got all the ingredients last night.

Jaime says we can all go swimming tomorrow at her neighborhood pool.

Awesome!

Kacey loves swimming.

x

103

Aren't you excited about the party?

I wasn't invited.

Maybe that's because Jaime just doesn't know you that well yet.

I'm sure if you asked, she'd—

I'm not going to *invite myself* to some random girl's party.

I'm sorry. When Kacey said the co-op girls were going, I thought—

If you're really my best friend, you won't go.

What?

I guess you like your new friends more than me.

Pof!

But Lauren, Megan, and Callie—they're your friends, too.

Not anymore. They're obsessed with, like, makeup and shopping.

105

They're still the same people.

BZZ_{zz}

It wouldn't be fair to cancel on Jaime last-minute, but I could ask her—

BZZ_{zz}

Poof!

Poof! BZZ

What about what's fair to me? Your *best* friend?

BZZ_{zz} BZZ BZ BZZ

BZZ BZZ BZz BZ

And by the way, it's super obvious you're still not wearing your necklace.

If that's how you feel about our friendship, then fine.

SNAP

You don't understand. My dad hasn't—

Whatever. Save it for your new friends.

I didn't know what to do.

I didn't want Kacey to feel alone.

But I also thought she was being mean.

I was having fun, but I also felt a little guilty.

Poof!

Poof!

If you touch the doorknob ten times, nothing bad will happen.

Your mom won't get in a car wreck.

You won't embarrass yourself tonight.

And Kacey won't stop being your best friend.

If you touch the doorknob ten times, everything will be okay.

one

two

three

Uh, Katie?

four

What're you doing?

Oh!

The screw was loose on the doorknob. I was just tightening it up.

Oooh, yeah. This house is, like, falling apart. Mom's doing projects on it all the time.

She says old houses are the coolest, though.

Yeah, your house is great.

So, ready for *Princess Diaries*?

Uh-huh, I'll be right there!

I didn't hear from Kacey all week.

I thought about calling her.

But . . .

. . . maybe she didn't want to be friends anymore.

Jaime, Lauren, Callie, and Megan were still my friends.

HA HA HA HA HA HA HA HA HA HA HA HAHA

I missed Kacey, though.

Hey, Katiebug! I fixed it.

Oh. Thanks.

Everything okay?

Yeah, I'm fine.

CLick

Maybe you won't need surgery if you count the trees outside.

 one

 two

 three

 four

 five

 six

seven eight nine ten

Yeah. I won't need surgery.

Poof!

I tried to focus on fun stuff, like drama class.

Katie and Jaime, why don't you come up here and show us your skit?

117

We got a standing ovation.

That's great.

Hey! Take a look at this.

"Fayette County Children's Theatre..."

FAYETTE COUNTY
CHILDREN'S THEATRE
OPEN AUDITIONS
The Adventures of Madeline

"... open auditions for *The Adventures of Madeline*."

I know how much you love drama class. Would you be interested in auditioning for a play?

YES!

A professional theatrical production?

It was a dream come true.

And way more impressive than some play at co-op or church.

Wait till I get cast.

Then who will have *actual theatre experience*!

Hey there!

Do you have a résumé and headshot?

I hope it's not weird that my headshot is a Christmas portrait.

POOF!

I was nervous. But mostly? I was excited.

Next up, we'd like to see Katie Ormsbee reading for Madeline!

I love to stretch!

And climb.

And rhyme!

Very nice, Katie.

Thank you.

He said very nice.

A few days later . . .

We would like to see the following young actors this Monday night . . .

Kevin Lee,

Jenny Nash,

Katie Ormsbee . . .

YES!!!

Callbacks were like auditions, only with fewer people.

And this time we were on an actual stage.

Waiting for the cast list seemed to take *ages*.

But I tried to distract myself.

Tick tick tick

BHC ANNUAL HARVEST FESTIVAL

Poof!

BZzz
BZzzz

BZzz
BZz
BZzz
BZZ
BZ
BZ
BZ
BZZ
ZZB

There were days when, if I was busy enough with other stuff, I could push the buzzing thoughts away.

BZzzzzz

But most of the time they felt like an itch I *had* to scratch.

BZzzzzBzzz BZzz
BZzz
BZz BZ
BZzz

The house won't burn down if you touch the cushion three times.

Turn on the faucet ten times.

Quick.

No one can know. If people find out, I won't have any friends.

BZzzz BZzzz BZzzz

At last, the big day arrived.

For audition announcements, dial extension 317.

We're pleased to offer the following roles to our auditionees:

Madeline to Layla McKay . . .

I didn't get it.

. . . Pepito to Mark Bellos, Genevieve to Heather Chen, Miss Clavel to . . .

. . . Puppy #3 to Katie Ormsbee . . .

Wait. I got a part?

Poof!

I got a part!

Sure, I'd be playing one of Genevieve's *twelve* puppies.

But I'd be performing at the opera house, where the children's theatre put on their holiday season play.

I was going to be in a real stage production.

I DID IT!

MOM! DAD! GUESS WHAT!

There'll be public performances on the weekend *and* school performances during the week.

It's going to be so official!

Congrats. That's pretty cool.

I was Puppy #3 this time, but in a couple of years? I'd be a star.

CLAP CLAP CLAP CLAP CLAP CLAP CLAP

MAD. CAST→

AAH! HA HA

WHERE JUST

HA HA

Hey! Welcome to Team Genevieve! I'm Sam.

I'm Alyssa, Puppy #2.

And I'm Jasmine, Puppy #4.

I'm right between you two!

It's weird, because we don't have any lines, right? But we still have to be here for blocking.

Blocking?

But we only saw each other for a few hours a week. It wasn't like we were best friends.

Not the way Kacey and I had been.

Not even my friends at co-op were BFF-level close.

I wondered if there was still a way to make things right with Kacey.

So it's definite?

It is, but I think it's for the best.

We'll be closer to my family in Connecticut.

Yes.

Jerry will start up there in two weeks, but we won't follow till the new year.

What a whirlwind change for you and the girls!

That's Kacey's mom.

POOF!

Connecticut?

Yeah, my dad got a job there.

I had no idea.

Why would you? We don't talk anymore.

Now, if you don't mind, I've got a chapter to finish.

Everything okay?

It's tech week, that's all.

Well, I hope you don't get too worn out.

CHILDREN'S THEATRE

Remember, we've got your dentist appointment bright and early on Friday.

BZzz BZz BVZZ

ZZ BZZzzz BZZ BZZ

How could I forget?

Tech week—the final week of rehearsal before we performed—was lots of work.

We had to rehearse every single night, and on Thursday we moved to the opera house to work with sets and props and music cues.

Whoa.

By the end of each night, I was pooped.

Katie!

Did you sleep through your alarm?

We leave for the dentist in half an hour!

One, two, three...

four

five

six

...seven, eight, nine—

Katie?

Dr. Kramer will be with you in a moment.

146

I recommend surgery.

I think it's the best path forward.

I'm booked for the next few months, but Vera will get you scheduled for the next possible opening.

My worst fears had come true: Dr. Kramer was going to *chop off* part of my tongue.

No, no, no—ow!

Sting!

148

The buzzing thoughts were getting worse.

One, two, three.

BZZZ BZZZ BZZZ BZZZ BZZZ

TAP TAP TAP

Are all your dresser drawers shut? You'd better check.

BZZZ BZZZ BZZZ

You have to check.

Ouch!

BZZZ BZZZ

SLAM

Turn the faucet on and off.

Nope. That wasn't right. Do it again.

Nuh-uh. Again.

Want to tell me what's going on?

I—I don't know how to explain it, exactly.

It's just . . . there's a right and wrong way to turn on the faucet.

A right and wrong way?

Like, I *have* to do it the right way,

or else I feel . . . wrong.

It's not just the faucet, either.

It's like that with lots of stuff.

And it's been getting worse.

I know thoughts like that are silly, but . . . I can't help it.

I'm going to talk to your dad about this, okay?

Everything's going to be fine.

My secret was out. Now Mom knew how weird I was.

Soon Dad would, too.

I felt like my mind wasn't right.

Just like my tongue wasn't right.

KNOCK KNOCK

Y—yeah?

Hey, Katiebug. Can we chat?

Okay.

Mom and I want you to know that what you're going through isn't unusual.

We think you may be experiencing anxiety and what's called OCD—

obsessive-compulsive disorder.

Disorder?

It's not uncommon. In fact . . .

. . . I dealt with something similar when I was your age.

Wh—what?

My thoughts keep me up sometimes, too.

And I do a lot of weird stuff because of them.

It's not weird. Sometimes our minds are just wired in different ways.

How do you know for sure that I have OCD?

I don't.

But we can find a professional who will.

Poof!

A professional?

It may take some time before we can get you an appointment.

Just like with Dr. Kramer, huh?

Yes. Like that.

For now, you can come to me and Mom with any problems.

Okay?

Okay.

This is so embarrassing.

I'll tell you something that *I* find helpful to remember:

Our thoughts aren't *us.* They're just thoughts.

They're neurons firing in our brains. They don't make us who we are.

So when thoughts upset you, or they make you want to do things you don't *really* want to do, remind yourself . . .

it's the thoughts talking, *not* Katie.

Thanks, Dad.

I didn't get it, though. My thoughts were my thoughts. How could some of them not be me?

And how could I ignore them?

I tried, but sometimes they just wouldn't leave me alone.

At least I had a name for the buzzing thoughts.

And that meant I wasn't the only one.

I wondered how many other people dealt with stuff that made them feel different.

It was strange how, when it was filled with people, the opera house didn't seem so gigantic.

You couldn't make out the audience in the dark. It just felt like one big, elaborate rehearsal.

Except for the parts when people laughed or clapped.

Poo, poo.

HA HA HA HA HA HA HA HA HA HA HA

CLAP CLAP WHOO! CLAP CLAP

We did it!

Some of my co-op friends came to opening night.

It was sooo good!

You all were super-convincing puppies.

Thanks!

Kacey wasn't there, though.

She was probably getting ready for her big move in January.

They should've called it a *holiday wrapping* party.

Missed opportunity.

I'm really going to miss you all.

Yeah. Team Genevieve forever.

But we've got each other's phone numbers!

We'll stay in touch.

And maybe we'll be in more plays together.

I still saw my co-op friends.

But the truth was, I wasn't close with any of them the way I had been with Kacey.

Our fight seemed so silly now.

That Friday, on our last co-op day before winter break . . .

Did you hear?

Kacey and her family moved early.

Kacey's gone.

I didn't get the chance to say goodbye.

What if she hates me?

What if she goes on hating me forever?

BHC HOLIDAY PARTY

I should've apologized, and now it's too late . . .

179

It was a new year.

But mostly . . .

. . . life stayed the same.

Estoy cansada.

Quiero azúcar.

Sí, por favor.

I *did* have two big appointments coming up, though.

JANUARY

Katie's Lingual Frenectomy 24

Katie's appt with Dr. Barnard 30

One morning in Sunday School, our teacher introduced a new student.

Everyone, this is Geneva Pasquel.

She and her family just moved here from Michigan.

You can call me Ginni.

I didn't have any good friends at church.

giggle

But Ginni seemed nice.

I'm Katie.

Hi.

186

Hi.

Oh my gosh, I *love* your hair.

Is it naturally red?

O-oh, yes.

Well, of course! Silly me. You can tell, because your eyebrows are so light.

It's just divine. Like Rita Hayworth's.

Do you know Rita Hayworth?

Oh. No?

I'm *obsessed* with old Hollywood actresses.

My icon is Audrey Hepburn. One day, once Mama approves, I'm going to get my hair cut like hers.

Way up here.

I think that'd look good on you.

Well, Mama says I have the chin for it.

But for now, I'm going with more of an Elizabeth Taylor look.

I don't really like my haircut.

Oh, but it's pretty!

It looks like you girls are getting along well.

Absolutely.

Mr. and Mrs. Pasquel have been telling us that they also homeschool.

And they've moved in just down the street from us.

That's so cool.

You're here!

Ginni's been so boring all morning, reading her book.

I'm almost finished with this chapter.

ANNE of GREEN GABLES

She's always saying that.

Anyway, I thought we could watch a movie together, if you want.

Have you ever seen *Calamity Jane*?

Um... no?

Oh, well, that's perfect! It'll be new to you.

I mean, if you *feel* like watching a musical.

How do you feel about musicals?

CLAP CLAP

Poof

I love them.

I also love *Anne of Green Gables.*

Really?

Yeah! The movie is great, too.

Oooh, we should watch it together next time!

Next time!

It was so fun hanging out with Ginni and Amalie.

I just blew in from the Windy City!

Ginni was quiet, but we talked about our favorite books.

Roll of Thunder Hear My Cry
THE BLACK CAULDRON
THE GIVER
BRIDGE to TERABITHIA
Jacob Have I Loved

Amalie talked a *lot*. About old movies and musicals and fashion and makeup.

This shade is called Cerulean Sea. Doesn't that sound delicious?

Cerulean Sea.

What's your favorite musical?

Definitely *Annie.*

Thanks for having me over!

Mama will make crepes next time, okay?

And we'll have a tea party!

It's a time-honored tradition in the Pasquel home.

Sounds great!

I really like them.

Good!

Because I *think* Mrs. Pasquel is going to enroll them in the co-op next school year.

Three days till my surgery.

BZZzz

I can't believe that's going to be *gone* soon.

Poof

M

Poof

Mom said Dr. Kramer will give me a shot in the mouth.

BZZzz

BZZ

BZZ

BZZ

BZZ

A SHOT.

IN THE MOUTH.

And I'll be awake for the whole thing.

BZ BZzz BZZz BZZZz

TAP TAP TAP TAP TAP
one two three

And they'll have to sew stitches under my tongue.

TAP TAP TAP

one two three four five

I don't talk funny. I can still eat food. Why do I even need surgery?

197

It's not fair.

It just isn't.

SMACK!

I dunno.

You look sad about something.

You'll understand when you're older.

Yeah, guess so.

It's just . . . I had this friend who turned out to be *not* a great friend.

Really?

What'd she do?

I don't want to talk details.

Oh.

I lost a friend, too.

It was kind of the worst.

It *still* is.

Yeah.

I know what you mean.

So I guess that doesn't get better, even when you're older?

Doesn't seem to.

Because you don't hang out with me anymore.

And you have your own bathroom now, so you don't have to be around me.

BZzz

BZz

I don't think you're a little kid.

You're just ...

younger.

One day you'll get it.

I wish I knew what "it" was.

203

Hey. About your surgery?

I know it's scary.

But it's going to be okay.

Really?

It's going to be all right.

Dr. Kramer said I can sit in the room for the procedure.

But what can Dad do if something goes wrong?

Or if Dr. Kramer snips too far?

I sure felt like I did, though.

One, two . . .

Still. It was nice to know I could *tell* myself the buzzing thoughts weren't the real Katie.

three four five

Poof!

That was a first.

All righty!

Do you remember Donna from last time?

She'll be helping us out today.

Good morning, Katie.

Before we begin, I want to be sure you understand the procedure.

First, we'll be numbing your mouth with a shot.

Then we'll be removing that string beneath your tongue—

the lingual frenulum.

Once that string is gone, we'll sew a few stitches.

And these are very cool stitches.

They'll dissolve over time, right in your mouth.

Does all that make sense?

Y—yes.

My parents told me what to expect.

Great! Any questions for me?

BZzzz BZzz

Will it hurt a lot?

Will you accidentally cut off my tongue???

What if something goes wrong??

BZzz

I'm good.

BZZ BZZZ BZZZ

All righty, then! First comes the shot.

It's okay if you want to close your eyes.

BZZZN BZZZ

The shot *definitely* hurt.

But not as much as I thought it would.

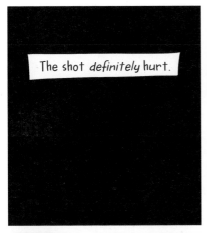

It was weird, watching Dr. Kramer and Donna work on my mouth.

But also kind of . . . cool?

Everything was going well until . . .

SNIP!!

Is Dad okay?

213

All done. Say goodbye, lingual frenulum!

This girl deserves plenty of ice cream.

It turned out that Dad *had* puked.

I normally have a strong stomach. I guess it's different when it comes to my daughter.

giggle

It was weird getting used to my mouth.

I had to stop myself from running my tongue along the stitches all the time.

nudge

But it was over. I'd done it!

No more buzzing thoughts about my lingual frenectomy *ever.*

I wonder what you're up to in Connecticut.

I wish I'd said sorry.

At first, I wanted to stash the photos away.

Throw them away, even.

217

But then I decided I didn't want to forget that summer.

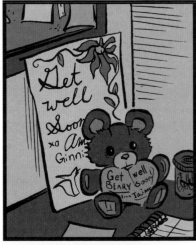

Kacey was still important to me.

She always would be.

As my tongue healed, the dogwoods bloomed.

School was almost over.

And as every Kentuckian knew, the first Saturday of May meant . . .

CHirp! CHirp!

KENTUCKY DERBY!
OUR COMPREHENSIVE LIST OF CONTESTANTS INSIDE

Ginni and Amalie had invited me to their house for a Derby sleepover.

I'd made my very own Derby hat for the occasion.

Oh, but your hat is *divine*.

You must dish about where you found this talented milliner.

Amalie made almost everything feel dramatic.

I liked that.

I also liked how straightforward Ginni could be.

They were the perfect pair of friends.

Now, since we're new to the state, you must tell us how this whole *Derby* sensation works.

This is our guide.

KENTUCKY DERBY CONTESTANTS

Now it's a matter of waiting.

And *eating.* Mama's going to make her crepes!

What do you normally eat at a Derby party?

Definitely pie. Sometimes burgoo, biscuits, and beer cheese.

And also mint juleps, but we're too young for those.

They've got alcohol in them.

Oooh.

Well, we *can* do this.

Ta-da! Mint water-ups!

What are you girls up to?

Making age-appropriate beverages.

Very clever.

Now clear out of here. I've got crepes to whip up.

They're our great-grandmother's recipe, and they're *delicious*.

CLICK

The Derby always starts at six o'clock on the nose.

You've got to tune in on time, because it's over in two minutes.

That fast?

Yep.

AND THEY'RE OFF!

Go, Invisible Ink!

Come on, Thunder Blitz!

MONARCHOS!

These are *so good*, Mrs. Pasquel.

I've never had a crepe before.

Never?

Well, I'm glad my grandmother's recipe was your very first taste.

Me too.

Mom says we got accepted into BHC for next year.

It's going to be so great to have you there.

And we're gonna do so much cool stuff together this summer!

Thanks again for having me over.

Anytime!

Want to hang out again next weekend?

Oh. Um . . .

BZZZ Poof

I can't.

My friend Jaime invited me to go to Kentucky Kingdom that day.

Will they get mad at me for hanging out with another friend?

Oh, fun! I love theme parks.

Is Jaime one of your friends from the co-op?

Um, yeah.

She's great. I can introduce you to her when co-op starts.

That'd be divine.

They didn't get mad.

Maybe I could have best friends *and* good friends.

I didn't have to choose.

And I didn't feel like a kid for not knowing all the "cool" movies and music around Amalie and Ginni.

I could just be me.

Poof

But would your friends like you if they knew about the buzzing thoughts?

HA HA HA HA HA HA HA HA HA HA HA HA HA

I don't know.

But I think they might.

The next day I had an appointment.

No braces or lingual frenectomies this time. I was going to a new kind of doctor.

One who could help me with the buzzing thoughts.

You all right, Katiebug?

Not really.

It's okay if you're nervous.

I would be, too.

But Dr. Barnard's job is to help you, just like Dr. Kramer helped with your tongue.

Only, no shots this time.

So she'll make my buzzing thoughts go away?

Well, they might not go away.

But I think Dr. Barnard can help you learn ways to live with those thoughts.

How to talk back to them.

She'll be able to help you in ways that Mom and I can't.

Whatever happens, you're going to be okay.

STE 102
DR. CLARA BARNARD
PSYCHOLOGIST

And even though
I wasn't sure what
lay in store for me...

...I was ready
to find out.

Author's Note

Growing up, I loved to read. Just like Katie, I devoured stories like *Annie*, *Madeline*, and *Anne of Green Gables*, which all featured kick-butt redheaded heroines. Those stories made me feel a little less weird about my bright red hair, but I didn't know of any books that showed what it was like to be homeschooled, or what a lingual frenectomy was, or how to better understand my anxious and obsessive thoughts.

The contents of this book—from Katie's trip to summer camp to her bad haircut to her struggle with OCD—are based on my own experiences growing up. However, there are some differences between Katie's story and mine. I condensed real events that happened over a few years into just one year for Katie and filled in the gaps of my memory with invented details and conversations that best captured my remembered experience. I also changed the real-life names of everyone in the novel but mine, to protect their privacy and because this is just my story, from my perspective. The

characters in Katie's
story were inspired
by wonderfully
multidimensional people,
and I can't possibly do
justice to any of them
through this single lens
of a story.

Younger me with braces on my four front teeth.

While Katie sees
a mental health
professional at the
end of the novel,
I didn't see a therapist until I was a senior in high school.
I was nervous about going to that first appointment, even
at seventeen. No one I knew talked much about mental health,
and I felt the same way about therapy as I'd once felt about
my OCD: that I was alone, and no one else got what I was going
through. But . . . that wasn't true! My therapist was kind and
knowledgeable. I found out that I wasn't the only one my age
with OCD, that my thoughts didn't make me a "freak," and that
there's absolutely nothing strange about seeing a therapist.
In fact, doing so made my life a whole lot better.

People can experience obsessive-compulsive disorder in lots
of different ways and with varying degrees of intensity. How
my OCD manifested and how I responded to it might be very
different from someone else's experience. Here are a few things
OCD isn't, though: *Just being really clean and organized. Just*

being a "germaphobe." Just being very particular. Sometimes people refer to these behaviors or traits as "OCD" without knowing what OCD means. It can be confusing to hear folks talk like that! Fortunately, there are many *unconfusing* resources out there to help you better understand your mental health, including the International OCD Foundation (iocdf.org) and the Anxiety and Depression Association of America (adaa.org).

I'll be honest: Writing *Growing Pangs* was a little scary for me. I was writing about my own life, after all! But I wanted to tell a story I wish I'd had when I was Katie's age, which showed how completely normal it is to go through changing friendships, to get unexpected dental procedures, and to experience what

Younger me rockin' on the piano. My hair had grown out
a little here since that awful haircut.

I call my "buzzing thoughts." And it's okay to reach out to
someone when you need help. You can tell a parent or trusted
adult about what you're going through, and together you can
decide what's best to do, which might include—like it did for
me!—seeing a licensed mental health professional.

If you're experiencing something that makes you feel
different from everyone else, please know that you're not
alone. There are others who have gone through or are going
through similar things, and there are people who can
understand and help, from friends to family members to
teachers to other trusted adults. You deserve the chance
to tell your own important, valuable story, and you deserve
to be heard!

ARTIST'S NOTE! BY MOLLY BROOKS

Hi there! I'm Molly. I drew the pictures in this book.

And even though Katie's story isn't MY story...

it's ACTUALLY pretty similar to mine.

12-YEAR-OLD MOLLY

- Bad haircut
- Braces
- Loves books
- OCD

Scully, cat #1

Cardigan, cat #2

The things Katie does because the buzzing thoughts are telling her she HAS to do them are called **COMPULSIONS**

OBSESSIVE (over and over)

COMPULSIVE (have to do it)

DISORDER (causes you problems)

I had those, too. But I didn't picture them as bees—

I imagined there were strings attached to me that no one else could see.

BUT THEY **PULLED** AT ME.

If I wanted to go in one direction, but the strings were pulling me in a different direction...

Dad   Mom   Eric

I had to do a complicated series of movements to rearrange the strings, so I would have enough slack to go where I wanted to.

① ② ③ ④

Coming!

If I didn't do it right, the strings would get tighter and tighter, the more I tried to go against them.

Hrk!

MAYBE THEY WOULD TANGLE.

MAYBE THEY WOULD **SNAP.**

Thunk!

OR MAYBE THEY WOULD PULL ME APART.

IT WAS REALLY SCARY.

SO I ALWAYS FOLLOWED THE STRINGS, AND I TRIED TO KEEP IT A SECRET.

BECAUSE I WAS EMBARRASSED ABOUT HOW WEIRD IT WAS, AND OF HOW SCARED I WAS.

BUT EVENTUALLY I FOUND A THERAPIST, AND SHE HELPED.

LATER I STARTED TAKING MEDICINE, AND THAT HELPED, TOO.

I LEARNED HOW TO MAKE THE STRINGS LONGER,

THEN WEAKER,

THEN EVEN TO IGNORE THEM COMPLETELY.

SO IF YOU HAVE STRINGS— OR BUZZING THOUGHTS, OR ANYTHING LIKE THAT— YOU DON'T HAVE TO BE SCARED, AND YOU DON'T HAVE TO KEEP IT A SECRET.

THERE ARE WAYS TO MAKE IT BETTER, AND PEOPLE WHO WANT TO HELP YOU.

Phoebe, cat #3

END.

Acknowledgments

All my thanks to Beth Phelan, who first suggested the idea of writing a graphic novel—something I hadn't thought possible before. You championed Katie's story from beginning to end, and I'm both grateful and gobsmacked to be on our *eighth* book together. Thank you, too, to the marvelous folks at Gallt & Zacker for your ongoing help and support.

My endless thanks to Shana Corey and Polo Orozco, an editorial dream team. I knew from the moment you shared your own magnificent childhood photos with me that you were going to take the best care of Katie's story. Thank you for your incisive edits and important questions, your compassion and care, your wit and humor, and your unbridled enthusiasm for this novel. You saw *Growing Pangs* through 2020, and that feat alone is parade-worthy. Thank you for always making me feel heard, understood, and encouraged as you turned my story into this graphic novel.

Thank you to Molly Brooks for illustrations that left me awestruck for 240 pages straight. Your talent bowls me over, Molly, and I consider myself the luckiest author on earth that you agreed to bring Katie's story (and the early 2000s of our childhoods) to life on the page. Thank you to Bex Glendining and Elise Schuenke for the stunning color you injected into this book. I grinned a mile long when I saw the first panel you'd finished, and I haven't stopped smiling about your work since.

Thank you to Dr. Julianna Sapienza for lending your expertise and tremendously helpful professional feedback to this manuscript. My thanks to both the International OCD Foundation and the Anxiety and Depression Association of America for providing resources that I have used both personally and professionally. And thank you to my therapists, both past and present, for the invaluable work that you do.

Thank you, *thank you* to the immensely talented Terri Libenson, Jennifer L. Holm, Matthew Holm, and Faith Erin Hicks for providing blurbs so kind that they knocked me right off my feet.

Many thanks to the brilliant folks at Random House Children's Books who worked to turn a color-coded Word document into an honest-to-goodness book. Thank you to April Ward for the gorgeous design work and to both Melinda Ackell and Alison Kolani for being copyediting heroes.